The Shallows

Also by Stacey Lynn Brown

Cradle Song: A Poem

The Shallows Poems Stacey Lynn Brown

A Karen & Michael Braziller Book

Persea Books / New York

Persea Books, Inc.
277 Broadway
New York, New York 10007

Library of Congress Cataloging-in-Publication Data
Names: Brown, Stacey Lynn, author.
Title: The shallows : poems / Stacey Lynn Brown.
Description: New York : Persea Books, 2018. | "A Karen & Michael Braziller Book."
Identifiers: LCCN 2018017953 | ISBN 9780892554935 (original trade pbk. : alk=. paper)
Classification: LCC PS3602.R72288 A6 2018 | DDC 811/.6—dc23
LC record available at https://lccn.loc.gov/2018017953

Book design and composition by Rita Lascaro
Typeset in Minion
Manufactured in the United States of America. Printed on acid-free paper.

Acknowledgments

Grateful acknowledgment is made to the editors of the following journals, in which these poems first appeared: "What Next," *The Birmingham Poetry Review*; "Valley View II," *Copper Nickel*; "Valley View I," *The Cortland Review*; "The Shallows," *New Southerner*; "Etymology of the Unspeakable," *A Poetry Congeries*; "Alternative Therapies," *Poetry Quarterly*; "My Father Finally Says Out Loud the Word I've Only Heard Him Think" and "Pre-Need," *The Rumpus*; "Imago," *Southern Indiana Review*.

I am forever indebted to Gabriel Fried, for his vision, his faith in me, and his countless contributions to poetry, and to everyone at Persea for shepherding this book into the world.

Special thanks to Bobbi Buchanan and Cecilia Woloch for choosing "The Shallows" crown as winner of the 2015 James Baker Hall Memorial Prize in Poetry from *New Southerner*. Thanks to Brian Spears for including "My Father Finally Says Out Loud the Word I've Only Heard Him Think" in *The Rumpus* and *The Rumpus Anthology* and to Melissa Dickson for including it in *Stone, River, Sky: An Anthology of Georgia Poems*.

Thank you to my colleagues, Catherine Bowman, Ross Gay, Brando Skyhorse, and Samrat Upadhyay, and to my students, past, present, and future, who teach and inspire me every single day.

Thank you to Southern Illinois University Edwardsville and to Indiana University for providing time and support and to the Hambidge Center for Creative Arts, the Key West Literary Seminar, and the Ucross Foundation for loaning me beautiful spaces in which to work.

Thank you to the writers whose words and kindnesses reverberate both on and off the page: Gabrielle Calvocoressi, Oliver de la Paz, Cheryl Strayed, Allison Funk, Suzanne Roberts, Erika Meitner, Tommy Housworth, Erin Belieu, Dorianne Laux, Joe Millar, Campbell McGrath, Sean Singer, Beth Ann Fennelly, Aimee

Nezhukumatathil, Rodney Jones, Stephanie Kartalopoulos, Patricia Smith, Kazim Ali, Ruth Ellen Kocher, Camille T. Dungy, T.R. Hummer, Gary McDowell, P. Scott Cunningham, Alison Apotheker, and Dan Albergotti. Thank you to Allison Joseph and Jon Tribble for their friendship, guidance, and love. And to those who left us far too soon—Susan Elbe, Ilyse Kusnetz, Vincenzo Tortorici, and Jake Adam York—your words are a gift I return to again and again.

I am immensely thankful for the long list of caregivers who have watched over my father for the past ten years and to all those whose work is to help others live, and die, with dignity and grace, especially Joy Gude, Kristie Akinwande, and Jeanette Mayeba.

Gratitude and love to my Indiana in-laws: Granny, Tash, Kirk, Rik, DeShea, KeShawn, Pops, Jasmin, Tanya, and Dakota. Thank you to the Westie Girls (Frances, Anna, Dorsey, Winnie, Robin, Julie, Libby, Sharon, Beth, Marlis, and Jamieson) for cheering me on and to Amanda Biggs, Kim Deckard, and Max and Miles, for their love and light. Special thanks to Joy Jones for always texting back, for understanding when I can't, and for offering to bring me soup. And to Frank Houston, for the stories to come, and to Lina and Jack, his best work yet.

My biggest debt is to my family: my sister Amy, for holding it down in Atlanta, my nieces, Morgan and Sydney, and my mother, who has shouldered the impossible, who has given and lost so much of herself, and who continues to teach me how to be a gracious lady and damn good friend. And to my father, Bob, tough old bird, for showing me how to stubbornly hold on to what is beautiful in this world.

All my love to my oldest and dearest poet friend, Brian Turner, who reads my work first and sees me best, for his steadfastness and faith.

And, finally, to Adrian, for everything.
And for Marley, my everything.

for my father

Contents

❧

How is life precious? O ignorant one, do not fall asleep now.
—THE BUDDHA OF COMPASSION

Dream in Which My Father Doesn't Wake Up

doesn't haunt his own life, the cat
doesn't wail my mother awake, sirens
dopplering the night, hurtling him
through one blackness to the next.

In which he lies peacefully
on the floor, letting go, whatever
light   tunnel   nothingness
comes next his, protected,

not protracted by rehab that won't
work, doors and windows soldered
shut, mutinies of limbs and mind
misbehaving, disavowing.

In which we say goodbye
graveside instead of this daily
diminishing, the slow erosion
of self swept out to sea

by waves that siphon rolling
in, spit carcasses ebbing out.

The Shallows

Valley View

At the top of our street, a cemetery keeps
time for the rest of us, its metronome of *dirt,*

tent, dirt more steady than any pulse,
a sundial sorrowing as the ground cycles between

the unturned, the freshly tilled, the blanketed
back over again. Groups huddle in loose

fists of black, bouquets of fake flowers
upending in the wind, sent skittering

to cluster in the culvert seep.
And each night, spots of amber

cast a softening glow, nightlights
someone thought to place

for the dead still afraid of the dark.
At what point does *mourner*

turn into *visitor?* Polished headstones
throw back the early morning sun.

A woman walks her dog. Or, no one
nears. At what point do we realize this

is no ending, these calls that always come
in the middle of someone else's life?

Etymology of the Unspeakable

As in *of insight, of*
midnight, of luck:

Movement against
a resisting medium. As

with a fist, weapon, or
hammer, the vigorous

dealing of a blow.
To pass over lightly.

To draw a line
through, to cancel

out. A sudden
or chance happening,

a fortune. A dividing
line as in dates, or

fractions. The blow
or touch of God's

hand. An accident
of the brain.

Alternative Therapies

The first six months hold
possibility, the prospect of

recovery, and so we research,
we wager, this one *hyperbaric*

therapy, pure oxygen under
pressure delivered to cells

that are dead or dormant.
Of course the dead will not rise

again, but the sleeping, the penumbra
of cells that circle the dead, stand

a chance of being awakened.
Muscle memory. Residual

effects. Crises of the body carry
with them new language to be

learned, to measure what has
happened, what was lost, what

hope there might remain. In the waiting
room, my daughter watches *Sleeping*

Beauty for the first time, wide-eyed
with wonder at the prick of the needle,

the swoon, the sleep. *Of course the dead*
will not rise again, but the sleeping?

I sit with him, our features
blurred through plexiglas,

and he works his jaw to clear
his ears like he did when he flew

his Cessna, trick of the pilot
handling heights. Years ago, I lay

in a chamber like this after
ascending too quickly from a dive,

the nitrogen bubbling in my blood
like words too dangerous to speak.

I know the pressure in the ears,
the hissing stench of odorless

air, the clear tube closing in
like a glass coffin. I tell him

he will be okay, but he knows
better, knows the story skips

happily straight to the *ever after*:
the turning of the crank

as they raise him inch by inch,
bringing him back from the depths

so we can wheel him to the car, return
him to the nursing home where

he will eat pureed potatoes and fall
asleep in the halls of the hollerers

while I shop at the store for food
for my mother, blinking against

the stupor of fluorescent lighting,
the overwhelming sadness of the produce aisle.

Imago

In the doubled mirror, the body
halved, unfamiliar as it was
when I was pregnant, elastically
expanding to accommodate
the alien growing within, only now,
I can see the fingers of each rib
cinching my lungs breathless, skin
stretched drum thin over bone. Then,
the numbers rose with my hunger for her,
desire eclipsing all fear in a ringed
luminosity. Now, even that light
dwindles, fades to a darkening
impenetrable, her rabbit fingers barely
shadowing against my black back wall.

Abandoning

In the
throes of
the undiagnosed,
I disappear
in increments,
tractable, scale
digits lowering
every day
despite the
carbs, protein
shakes, offerings,
a calf
fattening elsewhere.

My hip
bones razor,
the steppes
of spine
rising reptilian
from a
latticed back,
scaffold of
ribs, my
husband circles
my waste,
uncertain, my
daughter terrified.

Diminishing

(And when we were both inaudible, we sat
in silence, the unspoken tethering
us like string between two cans.)

First the breath, then the voice, words
husking bedroom, smokier,
vowels curled and beveled,
clotted throat, thickening, come
here to hear me, my whittled
croak so like my father's, team
disquieted
            interrupting,

                    dropped

every other …   …   seemingly lost …   …   …   …   sentence

…   can't …   …   …   soon …   …   sounds

…   wish   …   …   find …   wrong

      …   …   well …   …

                    …   love   …

      …   …   hear   …

            sorry

A Mile, Barefoot

Somewhere between Broca
and Wernicke, the road closed
to thru traffic permanently—
hard hats, erasure, stiff

fines for disobeying
signs that won't denote,
black-scratched hieroglyphs
wriggling like leeches.

Muffled sounds strangle in a
phlegm-filled throat. Severed
strings dangle dumb wooden
limbs, his mouth only half-

open on command no matter
how far the voice gets thrown.

Word Jumble: Aphasia

dreelcutt   __ __ __ __ __ __ __ __ __

carhacrets   __ __ __ __ __ __ __ __ __

rrgdeana   __ __ __ __ __ __ __ __

nda   __ __ __

rrgdeanaer   __ __ __ __ __ __ __ __ __

touhiwt   __ __ __ __ __ __ __

ginmnae   __ __ __ __ __ __ __

ignmgree   __ __ __ __ __ __ __

My Father Finally Says Out Loud the
Word I've Only Heard Him Think

Calling it a *rehab center* doesn't change
this nursing home, doesn't daub dry the drool
or bring the unfocused wheelchair-bound back
from those sepia-grained memories half a century
ago, gentleman callers in stiff suits clutching
bouquets they never brought, doesn't hush
the hollerers or still the worrying hands
of the woman in the corner who asks for a peach
every time I pass her, every day for weeks, until
the day her chair is empty, the day I stand outside
my father's room, listening as he argues with
the Kenyan caregivers, resisting their pleas
for him to cooperate, roll over, *please* let them clean
the messy sheets that shame him when suddenly
through the garbled spit of catfish that used to be
his language, I hear the word peal clean and sharp,
serrating the spaces between them, hanging
in the air like a curtain to be parted, and I walk
through, chirping cheerfully, smiling apologetically
to the two women who hurry out, exchanging
glances between them as my father looks up
at me with rheumy eyes I might mistake for tears
if it had been the aphasia, if the wrong word
had come out at the wrong time, unsummoned,
but no, it wasn't. Not this time.

Hospital, Rehab, Nursing Home Again

Everything about his care puzzles him,
from the oxygen tube looped
behind his ears to the bracelet
on his wrist holding hostage
his name. He studies the arrowed
bed controls, the cartooned head
and feet, the way he used to study
The Golfing Machine, deciphering
the geometric physicality of shapes,
angles, circumferences to calibrate
the most perfect swing, the way
he used to help me with my physics
homework, patiently drawing apples
dropped from buildings (9.8 m/s/s),
the triangulation of shade cast
from something tall. Now, I explain
the socks that compress his shins
at intervals, demystify blood pressure
cuffs and monitors, the blips that echo
him here, tethered. I am
the key to his understanding of this
world, cartographer of the known
and patron of the voyage, benevolently
blessing his adventure, sending him
off sailing into waters unchartered,
the rise of serpentine shapes in deep
space delineating the one thing he still
knows to be true, that everywhere
be dragons:

The Shallows

My father, wading out into the sea,
his pale legs bowed parentheses,
hair a dusting of once-black grey
above a body disappearing as he makes his way
into the blue green Gulf of Mexico.
Watching him, somehow I know
this is the last time. The ocean
telegraphs its gathering storms, lets glean
waters churning silt and sand as lightning
fingers the surface past the blinking
lights of buoy and barge, and planes fly
overhead, trailing their bannered ads. Why
these rough waves breaking him in half, not mild
like the waves he carried me through as a child?

The waves he carried me through as a child
lapped against my legs, broke on either side

of us as he shielded me from their spray, wielded
me shrieking with joy through the currented tide

that pushpulled our bodies, held us in sway.
Safe in his arms, I rose above each swell,

that moment aloft, descending gently,
then lifted high again. Past the shelf

of sand the water calmed, warming. Below
us, the silvery glint of fish nibbling

at his toes, darting unalarmed, the glow
of phosphorescent jellyfish gliding

past, their tendrilled arms no threat to me,
our bodies bobbing in the buoyancy.

Our bodies bobbing in the buoyancy,
my father taught me the physics of the sea,

that waves are disturbances caused
by distant winds, how they shoal
higher and higher in the shallows
until they break, or don't, while below,
the ocean floor erodes.

Always the question as we waited, poised
to catch the biggest wave back to the beach:
Rise above the cresting swell, or dive headlong,
let the magnitude pass through? Windmilling
our arms, we ascended like a prayer, beseeched,
carried forward with a grace that could never be repaid
while my mother watched the sky, called us back to shore, afraid.

My mother watched the sky, called us back to shore, afraid of the swell, the unpredictable tide, but we balked, swam strong, never worried about what we could not see, only the flutter kick of our legs, our biceps hammering through the foam, until the day my father, just beyond my reach, got caught in a riptide no signs warned us of, and panicked, thrashing to stay afloat while I recalled that lifeguard rhyme: *If caught in a tide that pulls you to sea, swim parallel to shore until you are free*, but he could not hear my shouts above the sonics of the surf, so I swam out to him, surrendering myself to the same deepening pull, cooed calming words, approached cautiously, talking him through, *Just relax, Dad, I've got you*, and I felt him let go, then, felt him frail and thin in a way he'd never been before, his concave chest so easy to wrap my arm around, his bony body light above my hip as I scissored us both through the unyielding waves, our chests heaving ragged with the knowledge of what was to come—the fragility of the future as certain to me as the grainy sandbar our grateful knees dragged against in the respite, the transitory safety of right now.

Safety right now means triple checking
the dump valve and tank pressure, duck walking
fins down the pebbled path to the water's edge, wading
ankle, chest, and body deep inside the darkening

sea through brown-hued blues and my own breath gurgling
dissonant in the cathedral silence, anemones waving
like truffula trees in this pocket of Puget Sound. Eyeing
me, a giant octopus lifts his skirt and jettisons, inking

dark the space where this predator spies. Halibut hoverfly
along the ridged and sandy bottom as I
skim the length of the continental shelf, just shy
of the drop off, all darkness, dividing line I now know

separates the salvaged past from future sorrow,
what lies ahead unfathomable as the unplumbed depths below.

What lies ahead unfathomable as the unplumbed depths below,

he	he	he	he	he	he
falls	falls	falls	falls	free	
leaping	through	in	ceaselessly	falls	
from	nothingness	the	falls	through	
the	into	study	carelessly	the	
drop	the	falls	falls	darkness	
off	murkiness	out	unconsciously	like	
into	below	of	falls	I	
what	tumbling	the	unwittingly	once	
ever	end	only	falls	plummeted	
comes	over	life	desperately	through	
next	end	he	falls	borrowed	
astronaut	over	knew	finally	sky	falls

He falls ceaselessly, carelessly, unconsciously, unwittingly, desperate and final.
Finally we come to understand that we cannot catch him, can only sit watching, waiting,

awaiting, hoping he will return to us but knowing he will not. Fasten,
fashion whatever is left over back into a man. The aftermath: stutter step,

steps listing, caned lurch, left brain, right side, braced foot, dangling arms and hands,
hand stiffened mid-salute, loosening his grip on this world one fingertip at a time.

Timeless specimen trapped in amber. Magnolia blossom floating in a glass cut bowl.
Bold, we take him back to the ocean, wheel him to the berm where the sand begins,

begin his recovery yet again, but his chair gets stuck in the sand, and he is agitated,
agitated, wants to go back inside, watch golf in the condo while his children,

grandchildren play on the bone white beach. And even though I know it isn't possible,
impossible, I still catch sight of him then, in the young man carefully making his way

away from us, disappearing gradually, that diminishing figure that can only ever—
never again—be my father, wading out into the sea.

Valley View

In the afternoon sun, a woman kneels
before a polished headstone, and at first,

I think she is praying, until I see
the tendrilled roots and clotted

weeds lying in a pile beside her. If
an offering is what is brought, what

language, then, for what is taken away?
Dandelions, goldenrod, yellow fox-

tail wilt in heaps. In the absence
of its owners, the cemetery

is overgrown, overflowing with fallen
limbs and ungrazed grass. And stretched

beside this recent grave, the unearthed dirt
still lies, weathering clay to a sunbaked

grey. Standing, the woman gathers
her tools beside the wheelbarrow

and begins the slow work
of taking away the dirt, of erasing

what has been displaced. As if
this absence could recreate

a presence, she digs her blade
in again and again, each shovelful a love

song, an elegy, an ode, each shovelful
a reckoning for the dispossessed.

Vitals

How many hospital
rooms, monitors, breakfast
trays, nurses' names written
over at each shift change, the hours
of ours at each other's bedsides,
arms needled, tubes taped
down, incisions at the collarbone,
abdomen, and hip, lapping
each other in loss, padding
hallways with gaping
gowns, with IVs trailing
like afterthoughts, our atrophying
legs beneath the blankets
palimpsests of the past, the shape
of things to come?

In the Country of the Chronically Ill

we recognize our countrymen
by the stoop of shoulders,
the ringed darkness of eyes
that number the years
without sleep or comfort. We
nod at the weariness in each
other's sighs, forgive the last-
minute cancellation of plans,
my own entry earned by
a four-year bout my body
waged against itself, war
of attrition, my insides wrung
like a spent sponge, cleaving
me doubled and rent. For half
her life, I tried to hide
it, but she could tell, learned
to count by surgeries, *one*
more day til Mama comes
home, *two* more scars on her
belly. Out of options, I offered
instead my unborn, surrendering
my possibilities—no more
pills to gauze the days, no
more swimming to the surface
from the murky depths below,
no more temporary aphasia,
the right word there, impossible—
until my cough, new sickness,
reclaimed me, standing

patient at the border, passport
stamped, welcomed home,
nothing to declare.

Diagnosis

Patient presents with chronic, unproductive cough,
pain in chest, unexplained weight loss.

I.

To name it gives it
power, dominion,
a claim of kinship.
Name it and listen for
the odds and anecdotes,
the friends of friends
and their suffering, arcane.

Say *bronchitis* and give
me meds that will not
work, pronounce *pleurisy*
and see me alabaster as
a Victorian heroine

parenting from the fainting
couch. Sign me up
for tests, specialists,
methacholine and PFTs,
bronchoscopes and MRIs,
laryngoscopes, esophagrams,
CTs and barium dyes. Rule

out *asthma, acid reflux,*
and *COPD* before giving
up, before passing me

on to the Mayo Clinic,
oracle of the desperate.

II.

Just like in Vegas, employees
at Mayo end every transaction with

Good luck, the wave of a hand closing
all bets, numbers clutched to chests

as we stumble chair to chair. No
seafood or prime rib buffets here, only

heart-healthy recipes you can find
in *The Mayo Cookbook* next to

teddy bears from the gift shop, talismans
and amulets to comfort and prevent.

No floorshow of feathers and pasties, just
pajamaed patients dragging oxygen

tanks outside to smoke in the shade.
And the sirens you hear aren't accompanied

by the clatter of silver coins into grateful
palms but by crash carts and gurneys,

the lifelines of IVs intersecting
fate. Croupier of the cough. Dealers

of pills, potions, and lotions. In some
eyes, kindness, compassion for the odds

the house has stacked and towering.
In others, the necessary, shrouded guard

they don like uniforms every day
for the work of making change for us dead.

III.

Ask again later, the oracle
demurs, so they take a wild
guess, red herring, rhyme
sensory with *neuropathy*,
accuse my nerves of over-
reacting, my chest presumably
working to expel an imaginary
pebble of illness. Which is to say,
they say it's all in my head,

the drugs they prescribe
a thimblerig where we swap
symptoms for side effects
(clumsiness, unsteadiness,
continuous, uncontrolled,

back-and-forth eye
movements, blistering, peeling,
or loosening of the skin,
confusion, convulsions, coma
and dizziness, delusions,
dementia, hoarseness or loss
of strength, congestion,
earache, difficulty
breathing, impaired
vision, indigestion, increased
sensitivity to touch, thirst,
gas, tightness in the chest,
trouble sleeping, trouble
swallowing, trouble
finding words). I drive instead

to Florida, where the salt
air hinges open my rusted
chest like a church key,
color blossoming my
cheeks, my voice returning

full throated until I
unpack back in Bloomington,
where the child sits heavy
on my chest once more,
my labored breath drawn
through a kinked
straw. They tell me

this is good news, how there
are more tests they can run.

IV.

Twenty-seven things
in the environment
to blame, the patchworked
grid of pricked red skin
rising angrily against
ten types of grasses, seven
kinds of trees, plants,
molds, feathers, ferrets,
cats, raccoons, the family
dog. The body's wholesale
rejection of a place.
Easy enough, they say,
to manage, just avoid
context. Nature. And any
urge you may still have
to breathe this world in deep.

Pre-Need

In the same
cemetery where
Uncle Remus lies,
my father's crypt
awaits, his mother,
father, sister already
lined up like cutlery
in drawers. The last
time I was there, we
didn't so much bury
as insert the body
of my aunt like mail
into the slot below
my grandfather and his
wife, missives to be
filed chronologically.

Not that the posed
bonescatter beneath
the dirt is any less
unsettling, but soil
at least thrums, teeming
with life. These stone
chests stand stoic,
my parents' end
parentheses. Card
catalog with body
of work, with bodies
unworking. Velvet-
lined jewelry box.

Night deposit to be
made where the marble-
cooled family bones
in residence abide.

Child's Play

Just yesterday, ringed circles, sweaty
palms, *Ashes, ashes, we all fall*
down goes Uncle Dan with his smoldering
cigarette and single malt, *Red Rover,*
Red Rover, Claude Murphy runs over
like he did on the beach at Iwo
Jima, weapon high, *Go Fish* his oldest
friend from the bottom of the boat-blessed sea.

Mother, Father, Sister have already gone
inside, the late day dusking streetlamps
aglow. Just one more game, just one last
name, Uncle Bud dropping the needle
in the nursing home. And when the weasel
finally goes *Pop,* stops, only Bob will be
left, always already sitting in his chair.

My Father in His Armchair Awakens

from dreams where he hears people crying
for help, adamant, he will not be
assuaged by claims he cannot
confirm, so loud and real are their pleas,
and so he must begin his slow shuffle
step drag plod to the kitchen, to the garage,
to the glassed-in sun room, and I wonder if

in his dreams he is as he used to be,
loping lanky-armed and grinning,
always arriving just in time to help,
and provide for, and fix, the way he still
appears in my dreams, a him-now version
that will never be, opening his mouth
to speak easily summoned words only to have
dawn break him back once more into
the silence of his stunned fortune.

Longevity

The will to live can far outlast
the body's tempered shell,
the ongoing suicide of cells,
stiffening vessels, a pacemaker taking
over the weight and work, his heart
happy to take a break for a few
arrhythmic beats. His vision clouds,
cataracts calcifying eyes
that have guided planes, puzzled
over blueprints, sighted the triangular
heads of cottonmouths peeking
up from ponds. Now, he moves
by memory, form giving way to
shadow, his already-forward motion
the only thing propelling him,
the way a dead flower will
hold its shape long after
it's been severed at the stem.

Exit Interview

What did it feel like, that sudden
lash, the smiting, being struck down?

Do you remember what you felt?
Thought? Saw? One minute you,

the next a twisted heap on the floor,
unable to speak, to cry out even

for help? I've heard that paralysis
happens like an explosion, flashpoint

pain and then the heaviness
of a felled oak. I've read

that when blood pools through
the two hemispheres, they

disconnect, and in the absence
of the chatter that tethers us

to this world, a kind of ecstasy.
In that silence, was there

reprieve? Did you want to stay
there? Were you yanked from

a peaceful place back into this
world, or were you stubbornly

hanging onto the ledge
by your fingernails the whole time?

Theomachy

I. Forsaken

And God spoke to him, saying, "Live a life of quiet duty and service, upright and righteous. Tithe each week, care for those who work for you, feed those who cannot feed themselves. Forgive debts that are owed, even though it may increase your own. Pray in earnest on your knees for those you love. Be humble, be kind, do all such good works as I have asked for you to do and great shall be your reward in heaven."

And so he did, and so he lived, until the night he fell and did not rise up again.

Though he woke, he was not awakened.

Though he wanted to speak, his words would not be formed.

Though he willed it so, he could not be moved.

Mute in His disapproval, he wished for a mercy that was not to arrive.

II. Forgiven

for not going to church, for not answering the call, for not blessing the food on his trembling tongue. For not wanting to be wheeled down the aisle, spectacle. For refusing to confess. For refusing his holiness. For never again bending at the knee. For refusing to give back a tenth of what is left. For refusing to forgive.

Do Not Resuscitate

If you come upon him
lying on the floor, unconscious,
do not kneel down to feel
for the wingbeat of a pulse.
Do not give your breath to him,
your turned head eyeing
the horizon of his chest.
Do not call 911—not yet.
Instead, palm smooth his
hair, his brow. Hold his good
hand so he can feel it,
whisper reassuring
things, like *it's okay*
for you to let go.
Like *we'll be all right.*
Like *you did well*
in this life. Like
we love you.

In the Vault of the Unspoken

Unsummoned
stories. The name
of his pet squirrel.
Answers to questions
I never thought
to ask. Punch-
lines. His sprawling
drawl. His first
sentence. His last.
The name
of his true love.

What Next

When he finally finds the courage to go to that closet, pry open the door, to balance the walker with only one hand, to make the good leg raise his whole body up, to reach without falling, without getting caught, to rummage the lockbox beneath the golf hat on the shelf next to boxes of slides, to nestle it smuggled to a room down the hall, to hide it from view, to wait til she's gone, til it's only the sitter, catnapping on break in the chair that was his downstairs, to unsnap the leather, work the grip from its case, to brace it against the dead weight of his hand, to thumb off the safety, to not reconsider, to get past the guilt, his old god, long enough not to care, to take the weapon, his life, at last into his hands, to close his eyes tight and inhale a deep breath, to remember his training, the triggered exhale as he curls his forefinger in the gentlest *come here* only to flinch an empty-barreled click, only to find that she's already taken his bullet?

The Depths

The sea we crawled from
only welcomes us back temporarily,

tourists tempered by cylinders
of oxygen on our backs, or

the urgency of emptied lungs.
In darkness that's never known

light, what's missing is never
missed, the unknown lurking

long before we noticed, before
sign or symptom emerged.

—◊—

What god is language if things exist
before we arrive to name them,

multilingual luminescence translating
the deep, chest pressure real before

we have words for *air* or *breath* or *need*?
Below and beyond, unseen, unmapped, not

the inert void we imaged but iridescent
galaxies of liquid space, a ballet

of bodies billowing, sculling
flocking and foraging in the hunt,

desire, or suspended between
this and *there*

not directionless but
incapable of agency, carried

on the currented will,
someday sifting down to feed

what hungers below, carapaces settling
to the floor, a sediment

unsentimental, the matter
of all selves to come.

—⁂—

What did we lose when we aspired
to live instead in air? We gawk,

map, hypothesize, capture images
and specimens to preserve, progeny

for posterity, to wield our time
worthwhile, arriving with all we

need, never enough to staunch
the flow, the slowest leak siphoning

until we have no choice but ascend
through borrowed black that lightens

from hunter to fern, jade to emerald,
refracted rays reaching like hands,

like a ladder leaning to be climbed
the last few feet and we break

broken through the surface, slick
with seawater, gasping

desperate as the newly
born or dying

for air in the ancient bargain
our bodies struck at birth,

our every inhaled breath
a ransom, a debt we must repay.

Dream in Which Someone I Lost Returns to Me as a Horse

unsaddled, trailing its reins in the sand loosely behind
like second thoughts, a beast unburdened, unyoked. His large

eyes invert me, his soft muzzle a whiskered whickering.
He will not eat from my hand but patiently waits instead for me

to figure out what to do. The last time I saw him was in a dream,
tethered to a hospital bed, unable to speak, those same wide eyes

terrified, imploring. The last time I saw him was at a poetry
reading, and when he stood to leave early, I paused and held

my hand over my heart, my allegiance, my pledge.
I unbridle him, remove the bit from between his lips, watch

him walk slowly away without a look back, surefooted
journey down the liminal line of sand, the border of two

worlds, between the berm that leads me back to town
and the slow drag of an ocean that will not let me go.

Notes

The "Valley View" poems are based on Forever Valley View cemetery in Edwardsville, Illinois, whose owners (National Prearranged Services, Inc.) took millions of dollars in prepaid funerals to fund their lavish lifestyles, eventually being imprisoned for fraud and money laundering. A group of concerned local citizens took it upon themselves to maintain the cemetery in the wake of the scandal and neglect.

"In the Country of the Chronically Ill" is dedicated to Joy Jones.

"Dream in Which Someone I Lost Returns to Me as a Horse" is dedicated to Vincenzo Tortorici (1967–2012).